Bounce, Bounce, Bounce!

by Jackie Walter and Beccy Blake

FRANKLIN WATTS
LONDON • SYDNEY

"I like to bounce,"

said Mo.

"I like to bounce,"

said Dev.

"I like to bounce,"

said Tom.

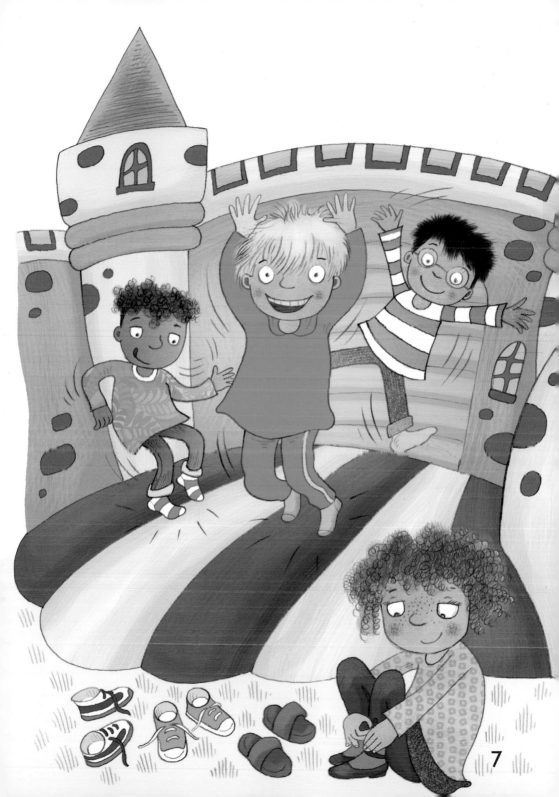

7

"I like to bounce,"

said Pip.

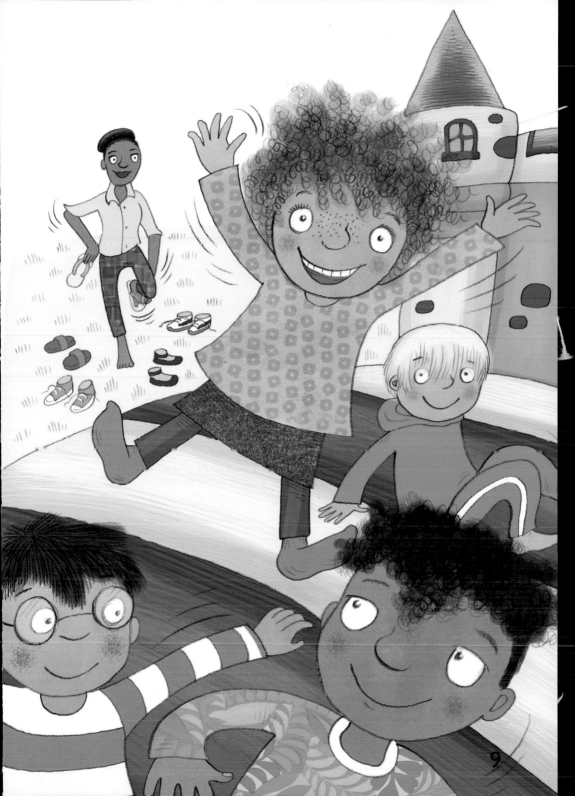

9

"I like to bounce,"

said Mum.

"I like to bounce,"

said Dad.

13

"I like to bounce,"

said Grandad.

"I like to bounce,"

said Gran.

18

19

Story trail

Start

Start at the beginning of the
story trail. Ask your child to retell
the story in their own words,
pointing to each picture in turn
to recall the sequence of events.

Independent Reading

This series is designed to provide an opportunity for your child to read on their own. These notes are written for you to help your child choose a book and to read it independently.

In school, your child's teacher will often be using reading books which have been banded to support the process of learning to read. Use the book band colour your child is reading in school to help you make a good choice. *Bounce, Bounce, Bounce!* is a good choice for children reading at Pink 1B in their classroom to read independently.

The aim of independent reading is to read this book with ease, so that your child enjoys the story and relates it to their own experiences.

About the book

In this story, Mo is having a brilliant time bouncing on the bouncy castle with his friends and family. Then the castle starts to deflate ...

Before reading

Help your child to learn how to make good choices by asking: "Why did you choose this book? Why do you think you will enjoy it?" Support your child to think about what they already know about the story context. Look at the cover together and ask: "What do you think the story will be about?" Read the title aloud and ask: "Who do you think will be bouncing in this story?"

Remind your child that they can try to sound out the letters to make a word if they get stuck.

Decide together whether your child will read the story independently or read it aloud to you. When books are short, as at Pink 1B, your child may wish to do both!

During reading

If reading aloud, support your child if they hesitate or ask for help by telling the word. Remind your child of what they know and what they can do independently.

If reading to themselves, remind your child that they can come and ask for your help if stuck.

After reading:

Support comprehension by asking your child to tell you about the story. Help your child think about the messages in the book that go beyond the story. Ask: "Do you think everyone had fun bouncing on the bouncy castle?"

Give your child a chance to respond to the story: "Did you have a favourite part? Do you like bouncy castles?"

Use the story trail to encourage your child to retell the story in the right sequence, in their own words.

Extending learning

Help your child extend the story structure by using the same sentence pattern and adding some more elements: "Other people or even pets might have joined Mo on the bouncy castle. 'I like to bounce,' said Dog. Now you think of one."

On a few of the pages, check your child can finger point accurately by asking them to show you how they kept their place in the print by tracking from word to word.

Help your child to use letter information by asking them to find the interest word on each page by using the first letter. For example: "Which word is 'Gran'? How do you know it is that word?"

Franklin Watts
First published in Great Britain in 2019 by The Watts Publishing Group

Series Editors: Jackie Hamley and Melanie Palmer
Series Advisors: Dr Sue Bodman and Glen Franklin
Series Designers: Cathryn Gilbert and Peter Scoulding

A CIP catalogue record for this book is
available from the British Library.

ISBN 978 1 4451 6759 6 (hbk)
ISBN 978 1 4451 6761 9 (pbk)
ISBN 978 1 4451 6760 2 (library ebook)

Printed in China

Franklin Watts
An imprint of
Hachette Children's Group
Part of The Watts Publishing Group
Carmelite House
50 Victoria Embankment
London EC4Y 0DZ

An Hachette UK Company
www.hachette.co.uk

www.franklinwatts.co.uk

FSC
www.fsc.org
MIX
Paper from
responsible sources
FSC® C104740